THE SCHMUTZY FAMILY

by **Madelyn Rosenberg**

illustrated by **Paul Meisel**

HOLIDAY HOUSE ∙ NEW YORK

For my brother, who helped
make the schmutz;
for my parents, who
helped clean it up.
—M. R.

For my mother, Marie, with lots
of love. (She never minded
when her four sons
got schmutzy!)
—P. M.

GLOSSARY

Challah: A special bread that's eaten on the Sabbath and other Jewish holidays

Farshtunken: Yiddish, for stinky or smelly

Schmutzy: An appropriate last name for this family. It's derived from the Yiddish word *shmutsik*, which means "dirty."

Shabbos: The Jewish Sabbath, which lasts from sundown Friday until three stars appear in the sky on Saturday.

Text copyright © 2012 by Madelyn Rosenberg
Illustrations copyright © 2012 by Paul Meisel
All Rights Reserved
HOLIDAY HOUSE is registered in the U.S. Patent and Trademark Office.
Printed and bound in January 2022 at Toppan Leefung, DongGuan City, China.
The artwork was created with India ink,
watercolor, acrylic, pencil, and pastel on Arches paper.
www.holidayhouse.com
3 5 7 9 10 8 6 4 2
Library of Congress Cataloging-in-Publication Data
Rosenberg, Madelyn, 1966-
The Schmutzy Family / by Madelyn Rosenberg ; illustrated by Paul Meisel. — 1st ed.
p. cm.
Summary: The Schmutzys are very messy all week long and Mama seems not to notice,
but when Friday comes it is time for everyone to pitch in and clean up for Sabbath.
ISBN 978-0-8234-2371-2 (hardcover)
[1. Cleanliness—Fiction. 2. Family life—Fiction. 3. Sabbath—Fiction. 4. Jews—Fiction.]
I. Meisel, Paul, ill. II. Title.
PZ7.R71897Sch 2012
[E]—dc23
2011040341

ISBN 978-0-8234-2840-3
(PJL paperback)

0722/B1225/A5

First thing Sunday morning the Schmutzys rolled up their jeans and went wading in the malodorous Feldman Swamp.

Mama Schmutzy didn't raise an eyebrow—even though
a little bit of swamp followed the children home.

On Monday the Schmutzys made two dozen mud pies and topped them off with Uncle Moe's private stock of Limburger cheese.

Mama Schmutzy didn't so much as wrinkle her nose.

On Tuesday the Schmutzys decided that tomato sauce made a fine addition to every wardrobe. It dotted Sarah Schmutzy's tutu. It spotted Baby Schmutzy's overalls and ears. Mama Schmutzy didn't *tsk* or *tut*.

Not even when they entered their "blue period."

And Mama didn't squirm on Wednesday when the Schmutzy children hunted for earthworms in Papa's vegetable garden.

When Izzy Schmutzy brought a bucket of the biggest earthworms into the kitchen, all Mama said was "Don't forget to wipe your feet." Then she went back to preparing the macaroni salad.

She didn't blink on Thursday when the children put makeup on Irving.

Or when they watered Papa Schmutzy's scalp to see if hair would grow.

Or when they decided that the pineapple wallpaper would look better with bananas, strawberries, pears, grapes, oranges, kiwis, and a leftover meatball.

And when they turned the sink into a natural habitat for frogs and other amphibians? It was Mama who plugged the drain.

Early Friday morning the Schmutzys played "Leap Over the Cow Pie" in a muddy pasture owned by farmer J. W. Lebowitz.

This time Mama Schmutzy raised both eyebrows, dropped five pounds of potatoes, and smacked her forehead. "Oy! Look at this dirt! You're *FARSHTUNKEN*, all of you! And it's nearly SHABBOS. We can't bring in the Sabbath smelling like COWS!"

Late Friday morning the Schmutzys
decided it was time to be not-so-schmutzy.
They unstuck and unstunk and
unswamped and unpainted.

They reburied the earthworms. They freed the frogs.
They soaped and scoured and showered.

Then they helped Mama Schmutzy braid the challah . . .
and set the table for twelve.

Friday night when they covered their eyes to say the prayer over the candles, their hands were clean.

When they ate Shabbos dinner, only two cups of grape juice (and a lot of crumbs from Aunt Pearl's apple cake) landed on the sparkling tablecloth.

And when they sang sweet songs to welcome the Sabbath, nobody thought about mud pies or cows.

Saturday morning the Schmutzys walked to the synagogue in shoes so shiny they squeaked and with smiles so bright they glowed.

Then it was Sunday again. The Schmutzy children grabbed their binoculars and went exploring. Just before lunch they discovered a puddle as big as Lake Mohonk.

"How many days until Friday?" Mama Schmutzy sighed.

Then she yelled. Loudly. So loudly you could hear her in New Jersey.

"CANNNNOOOOONNNNNBALLLLLLLLL!"